I0760529

Rise
Poetry for Lovers and Thinkers
HENRY LEE THOMAS

Rise

Cover Design: Nabin Karna

Cover Photos: Stock Photo Secrets

Other Photos/Illustrations: Stock Photo Secrets

Editing: Eva Xan

Printed & bound in the United States of America
First City of Publication: Manassas, VA
First Edition
hthomas@notjustformen.com

Library of Congress Control Number: 2022900874

ISBN-13: 978-1-970144-09-3 (Paperback Edition)
ISBN-13: 978-1-970144-10-9 (Hardcover Edition)
ISBN-13: 978-1-970144-11-6 (E-book)

POETRY / Subjects & Themes / General
LITERARY CRITICISM / Poetry
POETRY / African American & Black

Dedication

To all the people who are struggling in the darkness to find their way: look inside yourself to find the light. If you can't find it, then don't be afraid to ask for help.

To the love that was lost: thank you for the time we shared. To the one yet to come: I will always have your back.

To the people doing the heavy lifting in promoting peace, harmony, equality, and the common good: thank you for your service in keeping hope alive.

Legal Statement

This book is a work of fiction. Names, characters, and incidents either are products of the author's imagination or are used fictitiously. Any resemblance to actual events or persons, living or dead, is entirely coincidental.

We cannot move forward
until we start
moving forward.

-Henry Lee Thomas

Contents

INTRODUCTION

Welcome to RISE, a collection of poetry that touches on many emotions of the human psyche. These pieces are meant to be a ***buffet*** for your dining pleasure, an assortment of options and offerings for your consideration. You can pick and choose what you like or try a little bit of everything.

Over the last two years or so, we have been dealing with a lot of challenges, including COVID-19, political unrest, relationship issues, and racial tension. I selected the title "RISE" to help us rise above those challenges by beginning to think about them from a higher perspective and smelling the roses while still facing our issues head on and looking at them in a new light.

RISE is a state of mind, but it is also being used as an acronym for the following:

- **R**elationships: the relationships we have with each other and with nature.
- **I**ntrospection: to look within ourselves to find truth in our actions and our thoughts.
- **S**pirituality: gets back to being concerned about the human spirit as opposed to material or physical things. That is, to shift our priorities to the things that really matter.
- **E**volve: harnessing all the above to help us evolve into a more caring, healthy, and accepting society.

The first course is "Love and Family".

The second course is "Spiritual and Inspirational".

The third course is "Nature".

The fourth course is "Philosophical & Social".

The fifth course is for those with a bigger appetite: flash fiction/short stories that may be a little bit more filling for the hungry crowd who didn't get enough to eat with the poetry.

I end this feast with a selection of "*aperitif*" definitions, a different take on the meanings for several words that we all know and love. Check it out to see what you think. Maybe you'll have some additional definitions of your own to add!

Thanks for purchasing this book and I hope that it will provide you with the nourishment you need.

Here's to wishing that we all will *RISE* together!

I: LOVE & FAMILY

I Want a Poet for a Wife

I want a poet for a wife
so we can converse via narrative
and make love in free-form;

so we can both speak in epic terms
about our passionate union
and praise each other
with odes of poetry;

to experience our passion
in a lyrical fashion
as we dance to a ballad
in perfect balance;

to live with her in pastoral bliss
while reciting our love sonnets
and then nodding off to sleep
to soliloquies of respect and love.

A Poetry Love Affair

I do not know about you,
but I'm having a love affair with poetry.
It turns my warm body on
like I do not know what.

I have a physical reaction
when I hear great poetry.
Like having a nice glass of wine,
I get a buzz when hearing amazing words.

I long for my next encounter
with a love poem,
so I can get excited and moan.

I cannot wait to experience
the sensations in my body when
I read a nature poem.

I get misty-eyed while reading family poems
as I reminisce about the joy
my own brood has borne.

I know this love affair will never end,
and I will always get a tingle
from the feelings it brings.

Good night, my poetry love.
I look forward to reading you again
during the beginning of a new day.

Love Entanglement

We are in a love entanglement.
Whenever we come together,
we feel an uncontrollable force
compelling us to embrace.

I am in a constant state
of entanglement with you,
and I cannot seem to get away.

I want to leave you,
but when I make love to you,
I forget that I want to flee.

When you call,
I feel helpless to resist.
When you do not call,
my soul goes adrift.

You said you feel the same way too
which keeps us in this quantum mist.

Why is it so complicated?
I want to get away, but I cannot.
You want to leave, but you stay.

We are entangled in love, waiting
for a force to pull us apart for good.

Let Our Love Flow

Let our love flow
from our lips,
dripping from your breasts,
down your legs,
and into your love nest.

Do not fight the feeling.
You are not dreaming.
The flow and the glow are real.

If you do not let it go,
the pressure will build,
your temperature will rise,
and you will not be fulfilled.

It is a big deal
when we open the spigot
so our love can flow.

Do not be afraid.
Pleasure cannot hurt you.
So put on your seatbelt
and let yourself go
until there is no more flow.

I Love Music

I love music because it soothes my soul
and makes my body twist and roll.
It is a universal language, I am told,
when the sound waves take control.

The vocal and instrumental vibrations
combine to make the most beautiful sounds.
It stimulates the brain in the most glorious way,
making you tingle inside from the music that flows.

From jazz to classical, it's all good;
a smorgasbord of feelings and styles.
Our ears get excited when we hear a good tune
as we feel an uncontrollable urge to get in the groove.

Maybe it can bring all of us together,
united in our common love of this art form.
When you see musicians from different genres
banding together to make something new,
it sends a message that we all can use.
What we need most in this world
is for all people to come together
and dance to a common tune.

My Soul Is into You

I feel like you are part of me.
You know that you rouse my soul.
It is something that I can't control.
I hope you do not think I am too bold.

I do not want to smother you,
but I feel so much for you
that I want to cover you
with all of me,
even in my dreams.

It is a sweet thing,
and I hope that you agree.
But I do not want to go too far
and make you think this is lust.

For you are in my soul,
and I don't want to let you go.
But I will back off a little
to give you room to wiggle.

Keep this in mind if you will:
We have a bond that cannot be denied.
So please consider my plea
to give our souls a chance to meet.

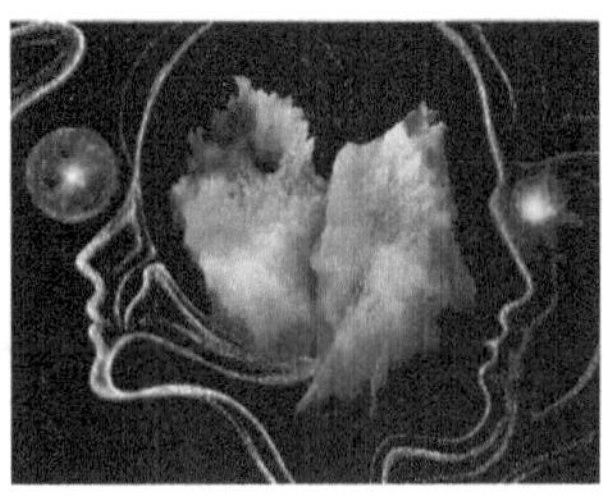

Undefinable Love

My love for you is so unique
that I cannot find a word to express it.
I feel the need to create a new phase
to accurately convey how I feel
when I am in your space.

I want to walk with you hand in hand
and dance with you all night.
I want to shed my inhibitions
by being nude with you in the light.

I have the irresistible urge
to pinch your cheeks
to make sure you are real.

I want you to move towards me
by performing a ballet glissade,
so I can treat my eyes
to your glorious facade.

All these feelings are juxtaposed
in my confused mind
trying to explain
this desire.

I am so happy to be with you
and I can't define what we have,
but I know it is real.

Relief

I need relief:
relief from the pain,
relief from the ridicule,
relief from the abuse,
relief from *you.*

Why do I endure
all this torture,
trying to hold on
to something that
does not feel true?

Taking a break
may not be enough
to turn things around
and find peace.

I'm so sorry for my departure,
but I need to make my exit
for the sake of my health,
but I wish you the best.

Don't Cry Anymore

I know you have been sad lately
from missing the one you thought you needed.
But crocodile tears will not fill the void
or protect you from the loneliness you feel.

Don't cry anymore.
He's already gone.
You need to move on
and feel joy again.

I know you are afraid of growing old
and losing your leasehold on life,
but you need to face your fears
and put yourself in gear.

Don't cry anymore.
He's already gone.
You need to move on
and feel joy again.

Please know that he did not define you
and you have more value than you realize.
It is just a matter of opening the door
and allowing yourself to embrace your grace.

Don't cry anymore.
He's already gone.
Instead, you need to count your blessings
and delight in what your future holds.

Flowery Lies

You have given me long and flowery speeches
about how much you love and care for me.
You put me on a pedestal and said
you would look at no other.

You said I was a rare flower,
with a scent as sweet as lilacs,
and a fragrance that matched my beauty.
You said my stems withstood the test of time
and that I drove you out of your mind.

You also told me that I was more than eye candy
and you admired my mind and respected my thoughts.
But you have been spending time with other flowers
and telling them the same flowery lies.
It is sweet that you have flattered me,
but that flattery extends to others
and makes my petals weep.

I will take my sweet-tasting flower
and move on to another fellow
who knows the real meaning
of cultivating my soil.

Blast from the Past

Running into you today was such a surprise
as we have not seen each other for a while.
I still remember the blast we had:
wine tastings and concerts,
frolicking on the beach,
dancing the night away,
massages for two.

Meeting you again has brought
out a nostalgic longing for the past---
happiness for the fond memories
but sadness that we are no longer together.

I have an intense desire to rekindle the fire
we experienced during our previous love affair.
Do you think we can reawaken that thing we had
and turn it into something that will last?

If you think we might,
let's get back in the fight
and turn our second round
into a permanent affair.

Poison Parent

A Poison Parent is one who slips
metaphorical poisonous pills to their child,
causing them to hate the other parent.

The ingredients in these pills include:
undermining everything the other parent does,
telling the child the other parent is horrible,
and rewarding the child when they express
hatred for the other parent.

The goal is to hurt the other parent
and to make the child love the Poison Parent.
Unfortunately, by taking this track, the Poison Parent
is throwing the child out with the bathwater as he is
also destroyed by this horrendous emotional sabotage.

It is difficult to undo the damage a Poison Parent causes.
There are no simple antidotes, and you cannot pump
this poison out of the child's throat so it will flow away.
We just must hope that with counseling, time,
and luck, the poisoned child will survive.

Heartbreak Hotel

Even though we would like to believe
that our love will last forever,
infinity may not have a place
in the human equation.

All our experiences are finite,
so they will eventually end.
It is great to enjoy the beauty
that love brings, but sooner
or later, we may end up
in the Heartbreak Hotel.

Whether it just fizzles away
or either lover finds another,
the only thing that can be definitive
is the love we currently feel in the present.

They say, "It is better to have loved than not",
but they also say, "What you never had, you
will not miss". Of course, how would you know?

You must decide what makes sense to you:
either experience the jollification of love,
knowing that it may eventually end one day
or stay on the outside like a lonesome dove.

I will take my chances with the former…
I want to experience the joy that love brings
and if I end up in the Heartbreak Hotel,
I will cherish what I had until the end.

Kisses

Your kisses lift me up
like an American eagle
flying high above the clouds.

When our lips touch, I feel a lift
and my love for you soars.
When our tongues meet
I can feel the heat
which sets my soul on fire.

I want to savor you forever,
even if I lose all my breath
from my mile-high love.
Please take my hand,
hold on tight,
and let us kiss and fly
together.

Your Little Black Dress

Your little black dress
is so much better than the rest.
It fits you in the right places
and makes my eyes go crazy.

You know how to step it up with
your black dress accoutrements.
You must feel divine in it when
floating across a marble floor
like a Hollywood movie star.

You have a stylish look
and you're a delicacy like caviar,
but the key reason I love you
is for the beautiful person you are.

My desire for you has no bounds
and I cherish you with all my soul.
I wish to cavort with you in your life
movie with you playing the title role.

My love for you is not a big mystery;
it's center stage for the world to see.
To show you, dear, what I say is true:
If you lost your little black dress
or decided that it was not for you,
I would still be in love with you
and hope you would love me too.

Love Spiral

I am lost in a love spiral:
I continue to go in circles,
trying to make you mine.

I keep following your scent,
hoping to get a glimpse
of your smiling face.

But I continue to loop
back through an empty trail.
You have left the scene
with no forwarding mail.

It's hopeless for me
to continue to march
around this barren space
without the benefit of your grace.

It's time for me to kick out this love virus
because of its impact on my health.
For if I continue to march ahead
in this vortex of one-sided love,
I will end up in a death spiral.

Love Elixir

I want to savor your
sweet, magical love elixir.
It is the medicine I need
to give me strength and vigor.

Your potent potion
makes me delirious in love,
makes me feel forever young,
and unleashes my fiery soul.

I want to drown in your waters
so I can be brought back to life
to experience divine happiness
from your immortal love.

Missing You

Baby, I have been missing you for too long.
I know I was wrong to push you away,
but I didn't want to string you along
when I was drowning under my own weight.

Now that you are gone, I realize my mistake
of not allowing you to help me in my strife.
Let me show you how much you mean to me
by being the person you always wanted me to be.

Please let me back into your life and allow me
to make amends for all the heartache I have caused you.
If you bless me with this wish, I promise to stay present
and endeavor to face all our future challenges together.

Isle of Love

We have been friends for a long time,
but now, the winds are changing
and I want to be more.

With whispered and longing breaths,
I enounce my undying love for you.
As the cool breeze of my declaration
touches the warmth of your cheeks,
I can see the excitement in your body
as you contemplate the possibilities
of you and I taking this to a new level.

I know you have been hesitant
to open your heart to intimacy
because you are afraid of getting hurt,
but now is the time to open that door
and join me on our little Isle of Love.

Bold and Restless

I am bold and restless for your love:
bold enough to tell you I want you
and restless for your loving touch.

However, it isn't a frivolous thing, you see.
For I also love you with all my being
and cherish every time we meet.

So take your time and settle your mind
and know that however long it takes,
I will be waiting for you for our loving date.

As Our Love Turns

Our love has been strong for a long time.
We have been through a lot
and always came out on top.

But times have changed and our love
is turning in a different direction.
It is creating friction as we adjust to the change.
It's terrifying to face the unknown…

We must decide if we want to hang on tight
or let our love drift away and find other mates.
It is a difficult decision to make given
how much love we have experienced to date.

I do not know how you feel,
but I am willing to fight for us
to turn our love back
to the right direction.

If you will join me on this quest,
I promise you won't regret the decision
because I will make sure to protect
and love you until my dying days.

Diamond in the Rough

Your beauty extends deep beneath your epidermis.
Your coal-fired skin hides the sparkle within.
Let me caress your body to bring out the luster.

You do not know how beautiful you are inside.
If you realize how unique and rare you are,
your light will shine near and far.

I am not trying to put you on a pedestal;
I just want you to be all that you can be.
Hopefully, when you reach that lofty goal,
you will consider spending some time with me.

Love Unplugged

Do not plug up that hole!
Let our love continue to flow.
I can feel the rush as we touch.
The pressure hits me so hard
like a firehose on full blast.

I think I am about to crack
as the tension reaches full impact.
The passion we are experiencing
is too great as all hell breaks loose
and we open the floodgates of our love.

Ode to Being Old

Oh, how we bemoan the tribulations of being old.
The frailties of our weak bones make us tremble
and the slowness of our gait is something to behold.
It can leave one to wonder why we are here…

We begin to feel that our best days are over,
but we want to press on like a true soldier.
We ponder if we have anything left over
and we rack our brains to find closure.

But our minds continue to stay strong,
and we have amassed a lot of wisdom.
Thus, we need to stop singing our sad song
and look at life through a different prism.

Forbidden Fruit

Luscious, sweet, and succulent
is the taste of the forbidden fruit,
the fruit Eve gave to Adam,
the fruit I desire from *you.*

I know it is not kosher
because you belong to another,
but I can't control my desire
and I want you and me to be closer.

I feel an intimate connection with you
and a strong relentless attraction.
The look in your eyes leads me to believe
that you feel the same way towards me.

Let's not fight the feelings we have.
Allow us to see where this thing goes.
Join me in our Garden of Eden
and let us feast from the tree of love.

Love Sensory Overload

I am enthralled by all of you.
From your head to your toes,
you rival the best Swiss fondue.

I melt when you whisper in my ear.
I tremble when I kiss your lips.
I crumble when your body is near.

With eyes so fine and velvety hair,
you are quite the delectable saucy dish.
A little seasoning completes your flair.

You are so much to behold.
I feel like I am about to explode.
I have a love sensory overload.

Wade in My Waters

Please wade in my love waters.
Do not be afraid to get in;
the waters fine.

I know it can be scary
to take a dip when you have
almost drowned before.

Rest assured that these waters
are safe and will not cause a wake.
You just need time to acclimate.

Let us take our time
and float around until you feel
comfortable enough to go in deep.

When the time is right,
we can move in tight,
giving each other mouth to mouth
under the moonlight.

Trust that I will be there
when the seas are rough.
Let us head out hand in hand
and sail away under our love winds.

Dating on an Empty Stomach

Don't go hunting for a mate on an empty stomach.
Just like going grocery shopping when hungry,
your desires will cause your logic to plummet.
You will go straight for the sweet
with the first one you meet
without getting what you need.

If you have been looking for love
before feeding yourself,
you will be too hungry
to buy what's best.

Take your time to love yourself
by feeding your soul so you are in control.
When you go hunting for love with a fed soul,
you will be able to shop objectively
and be picky about the one you select.

You should never be too quick
to pick the first person you see.
Instead, focus on the one
who fills your stomach **and** your soul.

Get Off My Wall

Please get off my wall!
You no longer have my ear.
I do not want you to leave any traces
that you were ever here.

I know you did me wrong
because I fact-checked you on Wikipedia.
I do not want to see your face on my Pinterest,
so unpin yourself from my social media.

It has been a long ordeal with you,
and I need to get rid of the clutter.
So, I am priming you from my canvas
and giving my wall a fresh coat of paint.

Poetry Is for Lovers

They say poetry is for lovers:
lovers of mankind,
lovers of the spirit,
lovers of justice,
lovers of nature,
lovers of life.

Of course, they are right,
but it doesn't tell the whole story
of poetry's impact on life.

Poetry tells the story of our plight.
From our joys and fears,
to our hurts and thrills,
it can all be told…

I delight in the possibilities love brings.
Pick your poison and dive right
into the poetry
of universal love.

Love Lullaby

Losing a loved one results in experiencing
one of life's most difficult emotions.
Whether it was a husband or wife,
child or sibling, or others,
the hurt is deep and real.

We will never forget
those who were so dear to us,
but we must find the strength to continue.
It may be difficult to do, but we must,
for we still have our life to live.
We will choose to honor them
by finding joy today,
as life must go on.
It is what they
would want
you to
do.

At the end of the day,
when you have done your best
to live a life full of love and joy,
think about those who are no longer with you
and all the fond memories you have of them.
Then, honor your dead by singing them
a quiet love lullaby as you fall asleep.

Paper Love

Paper love is the kind of love
that looks good on paper.
It checks off all the boxes
of who we should be
compatible with.

But it does not capture
many of the intangibles:
the soul, essence, or glue
that binds two people together.

Real love requires something
stronger than paper to endure—
something that doesn't easily
fold or crumple under pressure.

I sometimes think that
stone love is the way to go,
but maybe stone is too rigid…

Love needs to be flexible
so it can bend with the wind,
but strong enough to not break.

Lasting love has many seasons:
spring, summer, fall, and winter.
You must be able to fully enjoy
the spring and summer while
surviving the fall and winter.

If you can achieve the above,
you are on your way to
true everlasting love.

You Lift Me Up

You lift me up so high that
my head is soaring above the clouds.
My heart gets excited when it senses your presence.
I cannot wait to whisper in your ear
how you make me feel.

I am buzzing up and down
now that you are around,
and I find it hard to catch my breath.

When we kiss, I rocket up in the air
like a firecracker or a safety flare.

But I must be careful.
I can't get too enthralled
in case I suffer a hard fall!

Love Hurts

Love hurts when you
treat me like dirt
and do not give me support.

They say, “You need
to feel pain to know love”,
but why does pain have to be
associated with love?

Why do you feel the need
to rip the skin off my bones
as if I need to atone
for something I did not do?

It seems that you get a kick
out of making me feel sick,
but for me, it is not a picnic.

I need to move on
and leave you alone
before I am deboned.

How Do I Love You, Dear?

How do I love you, dear? It is impossible to say.
My love for you is strong and I cannot find the words.
When I try to explain it, the true meaning does not convey.
I hope the right words will be revealed one day…

I long to tell you how I feel so you will become aware,
but every time I try, the words seem to dissipate in the air.
Please don't think that my goal for us is to just have an affair
or that my inability to define this means I don't care.

My passion for you comes from a noble place,
but the emotion is too overwhelming to reveal.
I am so happy to be able to experience your embrace,
and my love will continue to mature when given your grace.

I hope you can wait until this thing is properly explained,
so you can understand the full breadth of my exclamations.
Know that I cherish you with all my heart and soul
and that I will always be here for you to my dying days.

Cupid's Arrow

My heart has never been pierced by Cupid's arrow.
Maybe it's because I have never provided a good target.
Facing the archers would have been better,
but I would be forced to face rejection if they missed.

Perhaps I'm afraid that love will hurt or that it would be
less satisfying than what it's hyped up to be?
If I do not open myself up to love, can it find me?
If it did not last, pulling out the arrow would be painful,
but not more painful than not experiencing love at all.

I guess I need to stop setting myself up for failure
and set myself up to be a better target.
I will choose to replace my fears with confidence
and allow the love-arrow to plunge deep into my heart.

The Shape of You

The shape of you is in my mind;
I can see your outline
with my eyes closed.

I can trace your hourglass figure
when you are not in my presence
because your lines are so unique
that there is no way I could forget those peaks.

How could nature mold such a perfect figure
with such artistry when the probability of success
is beyond my ability to assess?

The mold must have been broken
after you were baked because
there is no one else on Earth
who can knock you off your perch.

Your shape is engrained in my brain
and stamped all over my heart,
but I still want you by my side
to witness your beauty
with my own eyes.

Eternal Spring

Since I have been with you,
it has felt like eternal spring.
I feel as if I have been reborn
and rejuvenated to enjoy
all your pleasures.

You brighten up my day
like yellow daffodils rising to the sky.
The petals of your body give you a unique shape
that I am drawn to with heartfelt eyes.

I am attracted to your erotic jasmine scent,
and hope you do not dissent
from my inhalation of your
aromatic dissipations.

I want to hold you close
and toast you for the love
you have given me.

Hears to hoping that we will continue
to enjoy our eternal spring fling.

II: SPIRITUAL & INSPIRATIONAL

**“It’s hard to get out of your funk
when you insist on
wallowing in it.”**

-Henry Lee Thomas

RISE

Realize you are all you need to be.
It’s inside you, even if you can’t see it.
Seize the moment to acknowledge your worth.
Everyone else will follow suit.

Fire Yourself Up

If your life is not going great
and you think you need a break,
fire yourself up to change your state.

When the world is twisting out of shape
and fixing it seems to require too much red tape,
fire yourself up to set it back straight.

If you just want to escape
and you feel like you are going ape,
fire yourself up so you don't suffocate.

If you fire yourself up,
you will burn off the rust,
bring renewed energy to your core,
forget about unimportant distractions,
and begin to focus on the things that really matter.

Never Too Late

It’s never too late to love until you hate.
It’s never too late to accept until you reject.
It’s never too late to stay until you leave.
It’s never too late to swim until you drown.
It’s never too late to smile until you frown.
It’s never too late to remember until you forget.
It’s never too late to see until you are blind.
It’s never too late to live until you die.

The Change Within

When a river comes to a rock,
it flows around the rock to keep going.
When a chameleon sees an oncoming foe,
it changes its color to hide and stay safe.

When life throws you a curveball,
you may need to duck to avoid getting hit.
When facing a hurdle, you can't walk through.
Instead, try jumping over it so you can keep on moving.

Sometimes, you experience obstacles in life
and despite everything you try to do, you find
that you are unable to get past the barrier.
During these times, you may find that
the solution is to think outside the box.
Celebrate the change within!

Spirits in the Sky

Have you ever wondered if there are spirits in the sky
or a force you can't see looking down on you?
The truth is, there are many things in the air
that are hidden from our view.

There are particles too small for our eyes to observe,
and so small that they can pass right through us.
There is also dark matter and dark energy
that can't be directly detected, but we know it's there.

If you can accept the undetectable as being real,
why not spirits who give us free will?
Perhaps they are there to observe humans
and make sure that we are okay.

Some people claim they can connect with spirits.
If so, maybe we all can if we open ourselves up to it.
Maybe it's a skill we used to have, but it faded away
from lack of use or being told it wasn't true.

If we open ourselves up to the possibility,
perhaps we can rediscover a forgotten ability
that allows us to see on a different level.
But if we can't conjure up the spirts in the sky,
maybe we just need to rely on faith.

Castle in the Sky

Our time on this earth is limited
by the degree to which our physical body
can survive the ravages of time.

Through all the sorrows and joys of life,
our emotions are pounded by many storms
but we also experience enlightenment and peace.

We hope to find shelter from the storms
by having an extensive support system,
including housing, good health, and people.

We build our support structures to protect us
from all people and disasters that may hurt us,
but sometimes, it is not enough.

It may be that our existence on this planet
is just the beginning of our journey
and we will transition to a different place
after our final earth days.

When we ascend from our bodies,
we won't have to worry about
the storms, the crimes, and the pain.

So, hold your head up high,
be the best you can be, and know
that one day, you will be sheltering-in-place
in your castle in the sky.

Emotional Healing

Emotional healing is not taught in school.
It is more difficult to find a cure by design.
You can't see the damage with your eyes,
the symptoms are deep in your mind.

To release the demons in your soul,
you need to find the source of your woe.
If you were to do a deep-dive into your pain,
you might find that it originates in change,
allowing you to find a better lane.

So, experience your pain in this new light
and free yourself from its harmful grip.
It will dissipate from your conscience
and allow your healthy spirit to soar.

Everybody Needs an Advocate

It's obvious that babies and children need advocates.
They are far too young to fend for themselves,
relying on their mothers and fathers
to make decisions for their welfare.

But everybody needs an advocate:
someone to ensure you are getting the best care,
someone to help you make the right decisions,
someone to help you fight for your rights,
someone who has your back.

It's not a weakness to need someone's help,
so don't let your pride refuse a helping hand.
Allow someone who cares for you
to guide you through trying times
when you feel powerless
to advocate for yourself.

So, if you have a friend who
finds themselves in dire straits
and they have lost all hope,
be their advocate to keep them afloat.

Attitude Adjustment

Sometimes, when you are down and out,
you may feel that there's no way to get up.
You may also close the curtain on the outside world
and slip into a deep state of depression.

Remember that it's never as bad as it seems,
because you will never think objectively
when you are the one doing the evaluation.

Have an attitude of gratitude.
Look at the greenery and enjoy the scenery.
Make a mental cut to get out of your rut.
When you flip the switch in your mental state,
you will see that all you needed was
an attitude adjustment.

Silence

Silence is what the deaf person hears.
When the wild birds sing, they hear nothing.
When other people speak, they hear nothing.
When someone yells “fire”, they hear nothing.
When their baby cries, they hear nothing.

This silent world rallies other senses
to pick up the slack, making up
for the lack of that auditory ability.

Their touch excites all the neurons in their skin.
They can taste all the delicacies that man can make.
Their eyes can read lips and interpret one’s demeanor.
Their smell can discriminate between millions of scents.
Their sense of space tracks their body’s position in space.

It’s wonderful the way the body adapts.
It makes us that much more special.
It makes us unique in this world.
It brings diversity to the game.
Accept what is missing.
Celebrate our gifts.
Be content.

The Darkness Doesn't Last Forever

When you don't feel in gear
and finding it difficult to move forward,
know that the darkness doesn't last forever.

If life has thrown you a curve ball
and you are slowly losing your grip,
know that the darkness doesn't last forever.

If you are backed into a corner
with no way to escape,
know that the darkness doesn't last forever.

If all has failed and you have nowhere to turn,
know that the darkness doesn't last forever.

We are a survival breed who have persevered
through many difficult situations.
We also possess a spiritual force
that can guide us in the right direction.

Before you give up and go up in flames,
keep on pushing and believe in your faith,
and your darkness will eventually dissipate.

The Questions

We are made up of atoms, molecules, and cells
that are expertly combined to make a whole person.
We exist in this world via consciousness.
We are the essence of our existence.

But what is our purpose in life?
Is our existence purely incidental?
Were we put here intentionally?

The philosopher Descartes said:
"I think, therefore I am."
But who are we really
and what is our role
in an existential sense?

We certainly exist on earth, but are
we bound by its physical boundaries?
Is the 'self' confined to the inner brain
or does it exist outside of its human skull?

How do we wrap our heads around all this?
Once we find the answer to all these questions,
we will be closer to understanding why we are here
and the true purpose of our existence.

Life Going Off Course

If you find your life going off course,
stop the car and pull out the map:
the one showing where you want to be
and where you currently are.

Find out where you went off course
and figure out what issues caused that strife.
You don't want to make the same mistake
when you map out the remainder of your life.

Once you understand the issues causing this calamity,
you will be able to reroute your trip around the bumps.
Make sure you highlight key attractions on the way,
so you can enjoy the trip as well as the destination.

Life is all about enjoying the trip
and the people you meet on the way.
You also want to find purpose,
so your life can have meaning.

Therefore, refill your tank,
point your life in the right direction,
take a deep breath, and slowly push on the gas.
And when you get to some favorite attractions,
take a break and enjoy the view.

Online Church

Many of us have a church
that nurtures our faith
in the almighty God.

ML Harris United Methodist was mine,
even though I haven't been there in a while
since I am separated by many miles.
But it still nourishes my life
and feeds my soul.

I can now participate via online church
and still be part of the crowd.
I'm just not on a pew
sitting all askew.

It's good to be able to nourish
your mind and feed your soul,
especially when you are
losing control.

If you ever find yourself in a bind
and you need something divine,
pull up Facebook Live
and find an online church.

Christmas

Christ was born on Christmas day.
He arose from the dead on Easter.
Religious scholars debate the exact dates.
It's important that Christians celebrate this day,
So they can renew their devotion to Jesus Christ.
This is also a time for families to get together.
Make sure you are ready for this joyous occasion
And send your little ones off to sleep because
Santa Claus is on his way!

Turn Your Hate into Love

If the world is treating you rough
and you think you have had enough,
don't decide to strike back with hate.
Instead, turn your hate into love.

Don't make the mistake
of thinking you will feel better
if you raise hell
or cast a dark spell.

The thing to do is
to use that dark energy
to propel yourself
to a higher plane
by doing good deeds
and nourishing your brain.

It's all about how
you decide to respond.
If you respond to the hate with love,
you will pull the plug on the haters
and they would lose their control.

If You Could Fly

If you could fly, you would
ascend to the highest mountain
and nosedive towards the ground,
knowing that you wouldn't crash.

If you could fly, you would
circle high above the earth,
so you could see all the places
available for you to go to next.

Now assume you want to be
successful in some endeavor…
Fly high with the goals you want to achieve,
consider all the options for what direction to take,
make educated decisions on which way to go,
and then move full-steam ahead.

Being successful is normally
not a life-or-death situation,
so don't be afraid to try.
Believing that you can fly
increases the probability
that you really can.

Isolation

Isolation sometimes breeds
feelings of loneliness and despair,
but it can also evoke feelings
of reflection and peace.

This is the time to allow
your spirituality to soar
and to reflect on your inner self
without distractions from others.

Separating your inner environment
from your external habitat allows
all your spiritual transmissions to pass
across the divide without interference.

Take advantage of this opportunity
to revive your soul and jumpstart your flow.
Being in this zone allows you to be fully immersed
in a positive posture that transforms your frame of mind.

Nirvana

Why settle for a middling state
when you can achieve so much more
by reprogramming your fate?

If you want to be high on life,
eradicate the negativity
that is hampering that desire.

If you are feeling low
like you are stuck in a swamp,
catch a wave to get out of the gunk.

Set your goal
to flip the switch
and regain control,

to be in perfect harmony
with the mind & soul
and the conscious & subconscious,

to achieve complete balance
of acceptance, freedom, and happiness.

Once you achieve this,
you will find yourself
in a peaceful state of nirvana.

Conquer Your Self-Doubt

We have all had bad breaks—make no mistake.
It's a challenging task to keep up with the herd.
After a terrible fall, our bodies will shake,
causing our confidence to be blurred.

There is no need to stay in this state.
Instead, you must notice your dilemma
to lessen its weight.

Stop your negative thinking
and focus on all your glory.
See yourself as winning
and tell that story.

This will give you the clout
to rewire your brain
and conquer your self-doubt
to focus on your fame.

Pain and Joy

Pain is an unavoidable fact of life.
From birth to death, we all feel a little discomfort.
More so than love, hate, happiness, or sadness;
it's the one thing we have most in common.

We can avoid some of the pain
by taking preventive measures,
but trying to avoid it all together is futile
and is tantamount to cancelling life itself.

How we respond to this distasteful condition
makes all the difference in our attitude
and determines how and if we recover from it.
If we evade it, we avoid the chance of happiness.

If we think of it as a part of life and a temporary state,
we can look on the other side and minimize the heartbreak.
There is light at the end of the tunnel, so we must open the door
to conquer our pain and embrace our joy.

We Are Not Alone

Prop us up, Lord,
when our knees are weak
and we can't seem to stand.

Take our hand, Lord,
to pull us up the hill
when we have trouble climbing.

Keep us afloat, Lord,
when we are struggling underwater
and we have lost our ability to swim.

We will be forever in your debt
and you have our undying gratitude
for helping us during our darkest moods.

By your grace, we can
stand, walk, and swim on our own,
knowing that we are not alone.

Knocking on Hell's Door

Knocking on hell's door
feels very hot and humid.
It's not as inviting as heaven
with its soft fragrance and moist dew.

What door you end up at is not a mystery
unless you believe in no-fault living.
Otherwise, your destination depends on
the decisions and actions you make in life.

It's often debated if you can change your stripes
late in life by repenting for all your mistakes.
The questions are: "How sincere do you need to be?"
and "Are there some actions that aren't forgiven?"

I wouldn't take chances if I were you,
but you may be a risk-taker who lives on the edge.
Just remember that there are no do-overs
and too much heat is not good for your skin.

Peace, Be Still

Peace, be still and give me a moment
to catch my breath and calm my mind.
I know you won't be a lasting endowment,
but give me a chance to catch my wind.

I have spent too much time with misery
and it selfishly doesn't want to let me go.
I do not want to cause myself permanent injury,
so I need to find a more pleasant beau.

If you can't stick around forever, I understand,
but I will cherish the serene time we have enjoyed.
You will also give me the strength to make a stand
against negative forces to keep from being destroyed.

It is important for us to reset our state of mind
during the fleeting instant that peace is found.
Doing so helps us to leave our challenges behind
and allow our spirit to have a chance to rebound.

We Are

I am me.
I am who I need to be.
I am who I was meant to be.

I am unique.
No one can be like me.
No one needs to be me.

Accept me for who I am.
Don't try to change me.
Love me unconditionally.

We are all okay.
We live in our own space.
We all have a place.

On a cosmic level, though,
we are all one being
connected in time.
You are *me*.
I am *you*.
We are.

Caged Bird

Caged bird, please don't cry.
You will eventually have your day.
You will be able to spread your wings and fly
while not being anyone's prey.

Just bide your time
until you see your chance
to be free.

You are still in your prime,
so you need to continue to believe
until you can flee.

Chains

Your chains don't define you:
chained to your heartache,
chained to your history,
chained to your fears.

It's a state of mind
that's holding you back.
You are only temporarily confined,
so give yourself some slack.

If you feel you can't break free,
change your brain-channel,
project a positive mental key,
and witness your chains dismantle.

The State of Love

The state of love is not a physical place.
It's not a formal religion or spiritual faith.
It is a state of mind for humanity.

It's loving your neighbor,
it's loving your country,
it's loving yourself.

If we love each other
and treat one another as one,
there would be no crime.

Because a crime against one
would be a crime against *all* of us,
and committing such an act
would be a violation against yourself.

It's in all our best interests
to live by the golden rule
and to think before making a move
that ultimately perturbs our love-groove.

Drifting

I am drifting
along a path
in which
I don't seem
to have control.
Where it leads,
I don't know.
All I know
is that I am
finding it clear
that this path
is not where
I want to be.
So, I am finding
the strength
to stop the
current from
carrying me
away to an
unknown place.
And once I
turn the tide,
I will end up
where I need to be.

Take Care of Yourself

No man or woman can continue to thrive
when they don't take care of their own needs.
It's good to take care of others with helpful deeds,
but you won't last for long if you let yourself bleed.

Some say that the more you can help yourself,
the more you will be able to help others.
Of course, if there is a critical need,
try to answer another's plea.

It certainly can be a balancing act:
making everyone happy, including yourself.
When you are not sure what path you need to take,
realize that, if you need to save yourself, others can wait.

The poor people who don't heed the above warning
will end up becoming extinct like the dodo bird.
If you are in need and someone desires your assistance,
deny your urge to help and take care of yourself.

Endless Days

Endless days are passing me by,
not knowing where I am
or what I desire.

They all seem to blend:
one no different than the other,
neither one having meaning.

I have lost all my sense of time,
I don't know what's on my mind,
and it just seems like a daily grind.

It's time for me to turn this thing around
and to get off the merry-go-round,
so I can just focus on the beauty of today.

Good Morning, Lord

Good morning, Lord.
It's nice to be in your presence today
and feel the joy and enlightenment
that your love brings to me in my time of need.

Others may not be aware of the hope you bring
that will help them get through their daily troubles.
If they only knew you were by their side,
their fears would surely die.

Evil forces are lurking,
trying to gain a foothold on their brain
to convince them that they are in this alone.
Don't let them be fooled by these devilish foes.

Lord, open their hearts to your glorious force,
so that they can overcome their overarching despair.
For once they become aware of your grace,
their enemies should beware.

Know Yourself Well

Thrive to know yourself well.
Others may see you in a different way,
but self-awareness should rule the day.

You can't look in a mirror
to see the self that you want to be,
but it may reveal the self that others see.

Who is seeing the right you?
Are you the authority of your own soul
or do others hold the key to how you roll?

You must find the "who" that is "you"
and not the exterior one that others view.
Then you can make your own choice
and speak in your own voice.

Once you have determined who you really are,
the next question you must ask yourself is:
"Who do you really want to be
and what do you need to do
to create that view"?

Wisdom Is Not a Trait of Closed Minds

Wisdom is not a trait of closed minds,
and they are the ones who need it the most.
Though you would think that it would build with time,
that's not necessarily how it's dispersed.

It's the ability to have knowledge and good judgment,
which are qualities best served for owners of closed brains.
Closed minds obstruct wisdom from flowing
as they get bottled up in their confined spaces.

A closed mind is one with bias, bigotry, or hate.
They base their beliefs on fear, prejudice,
and untruths without any original thoughts.

Those with closed minds believe they are wise,
but they fail to see that their vision is clouded.
It is impossible for them to see clearly
when their minds are being deceived.
This illusion and delusion of truth
does not equate to a wise man.

A safe zone is needed for these lost souls,
so they can quickly expand their closed minds
to let in the light without fear of repercussions.
If they can achieve this lofty feat,
wisdom would finally reside
with those who need it the most.

Focus On Your Future Self

Focus on your future self:
the self you want to be one day,
the self who fulfills your future needs,
the self who achieves your biggest dreams,
the self you want inscribed on your graveyard plaque.

We all spend too much valuable time on the daily grind
while ignoring the tasks that will move us ahead.
If we don't set aside time to work on our future,
we are destined to remain in the past.

Where do you want to go from here?
What do you most want to achieve?
Who do you really want to be?
Focus on these questions,
design your optimal life,
and spend time living it.

III: NATURE

How Do I Love You, Nature?

How do I love you, nature?
Let me confess the ways:
I love you for how you tingle all my senses,
bringing so much joy and stimulation to my days.

I am overwhelmed by your palette of colors
and the different paintings you provide for my eyes.
It's a stunning visual gift for artists and lovers,
and I feel blessed that I can enjoy the glory.

Just when I thought you had no more to give,
you bombard me with a symphony for my ears.
When I strain the sounds through a musical sieve,
the art, beauty, and rhythm of it all brings me to tears.

I am so happy that you are all around me,
and I hope you will always give me so much joy.

One with Nature

I am one with nature.

My skin is like the Black Dirt
region of a Hawaiian beach.

My hair is like the Big Thicket
Biosphere Reserve region of Texas.

My tears are like the falling waters
at Frank Lloyd Wright's UNESCO
World Heritage House.

My body is superimposed
on nature's canvas
as I move with the wind
on nature's campus.

Nature

Nature is all around us, sharing space
with the brick & mortar and concrete jungle.
It makes up most of this earth,
but we seldom enjoy its grace.

We spend most of our time rushing around
without stopping to marvel at its miracle:
mountains and valleys,
oceans and deserts,
plants and animals;
all the things existing
before mankind.

In space-time, nature has always been here—
well before we entered this sphere.
Take the time to notice this treasure
and enjoy its many pleasures.

Grains of Sand

Searching for a solution
to the world's convolution
when there is so much vacillation,
is not easy to filter through.

Like grains of sand
in a vast desert,
it's hard to find
the right pebble.

There are sands of many colors---
sands that represent
all the lands
and people of the earth.

We must sift through many grains
to find a sustainable solution
that undoes the convolution,
and execute it with caution
in hopes that we can save
the world in time.

The Summer Rain

The summer rain falls
forcibly on my head,
causing my hair to spread.

When I take off my clothes
to enjoy the full effect,
I am enveloped in H_2O.

It's a soothing feeling
after the temperature rises.
It gives me relief
from the summer heat.

Big plump droplets
meandering down my back
and squeezing between my breasts,
give me the chills,
but it feels so neat.

To be naked with nature is not awkward
as it feels so nourishing on my skin.
So, I continue to surrender
until the rain is done.
Then, I enjoy
the awakening sun.

Head in the Clouds

As I sit with my head in the clouds
thinking about the world's problems
that are not practical to solve,
my mind slowly drifts
to the clouds in the sky.

I am resting on a fluffy cloud,
looking up at the stars at night.
The view from there is quite a site.
It feels like Christmas with all the stars
blinking and twinkling all around me.

I am very comfortable in this nature retreat,
floating around without a care on the earth.
To be as one with nature makes me
feel like I am part of a bigger thing
and that my life has more meaning.

But just when it was getting good,
a shooting star zips by my head,
causing me to lose my focus
and bringing me back to reality
in my office chair.

I will never forget my trip up in the air
on my comfy cloud and front-row seat
to the galaxy's many treats.
It was worth the diversion,
but now, I must get back
to solving the world's problems!

Red Rock Heaven

The red rocks of Sedona
are a gift from heaven.
They glisten in the sky
when the sun strikes their capstone.

They are a majestic sight,
showing off their morning glow,
but they take on a magical flare
when they are viewed at sunset.

They house hidden vortexes
that radiate mystical energy,
spiraling up to the skies
and down through the earth.

It's a wonderful thing
to experience the effect
on your body and soul.

So, if you need enlightenment
or want to enjoy the delights,
head on up to this spiritual site.
You will not leave unmoved…

Fresh Grass

Green grass has a lovely smell
after it's freshly cut on a spring day.
Add a little rain, followed by a bit of sun,
and it becomes a glorious sensory gun,
shooting out rays of grass-scented bullets.

A manicured lawn also looks great,
bringing the eyes and nose
into a gentle embrace.

Rolling in the grass is also fun,
but look out for those worms!
It brings you back to your childhood
when playing outside was the most fun.

The next time you are feeling down
or stuck inside with nothing to do,
don't just suck it up and grit your teeth,
go outside and enjoy the fresh grass!

Fireflies

Fireflies glow in the twilight,
emitting their soft warm light
as they get ready for a party night.

Thousands of them light up the sky.
If you didn't know any better, you would think
you were seeing the hazy band of the Milky Way.

They use their dim conspicuous bioluminescence
to attract mates to date and to devour their prey.
So, if you are a potential meal and not a firefly,
I would advise you to get out of their way!

It's Hydrangea Time

Many flowers have held the public interest:
roses are for lovers, peonies are for weddings,
orchids have a delicate, exotic, and graceful look,
and calla lilies for purity, holiness, and faithfulness.

But it's now hydrangea time.
We remember them as shrubs in the past,
but now, they can also be a vine or tree.
With their beautiful rich-colored flowers
and showy display, they are such a sight to see.

Their blooms last longer than a social media vine
and their flowers have the scent of a fine wine.
There are enough different species and varieties
to satisfy even the most discriminating palate!

Your cup will overflow
with the pleasures you receive
from this cup-shaped flower breed.
They can satisfy many of your needs:
they make excellent wedding flowers,
they are pretty in pink and other colors,
and they can bloom from early spring into fall.

Once you see all the benefits hydrangeas emit,
you will realize other flowers just can't touch them!

Air Affair

Smell the morning air.
Exhale your pent-up despair.
Love your air affair.

Let The Wind Blow

The wind is such a beautiful thing:
It travels near and far
without a care in the world.

It can be warm or cold,
depending on its disposition.
It can also be strong or weak,
depending on its temperament.

I would love to ride it
to the end of the earth,
to see all the wonders
from a higher perch.

I don’t care which direction I go
or what dangers may be waiting;
I will leave it up to nature
to be my savior.

So, I put on my seatbelt,
recline my seat, sit back,
and let the wind blow…

Babbling Brook

There's a babbling brook behind my house
that sounds like a brown-headed cowbird.
It makes a liquid-sounding series of gurgling notes,
followed by whistles as the water trickles away.

It's a beautiful sound with a constant beat
and it makes you want to fall asleep.
If you manage to keep your eyes awake,
you may wonder what is causing it to percolate.

Proverbs says a babbling brook is the fountain of wisdom:
wisdom that flows in rivers of living water.
This implies man can be one with nature,
if he allows his wisdom to flow within.

A profound partnership is man and nature.
Let the waters refresh your spirit
and bubble up the wisdom in your head.
But if you can't muster up that tranquil state,
at least enjoy the babbling brook in my backyard.

Sky View

Up in the sky, oh how high,
I'm drifting around like a balloon in the air.
I see cities, rivers, cornfields and more.
This sky view makes me feel
like I can forever soar.

It looks so beautiful up here,
observing the earth
in the quiet realm
of outer space.

I will continue to enjoy the stellar view,
but I will make sure not to float too high
as to reach the stratosphere
and not be able to return to earth!

One Lonely Songbird

One lonely songbird is lost at sea,
thousands of miles from her own breed,
and flies so high that she can't be seen.

Approaching a tiny island with just one tree,
this avian visitor flaps her wings with glee.
Hoping to land and catch her breath,
she glides in to avoid certain death.

This private oasis is a lifesaver
for this weary bird who has flown
for days through a dreary sky without
food or shelter with her wings on fire.

Through all her sorrows, she looks up
to witness the beauty of the desolate scene:
the orange-red sky and that beautiful tree
with arms spread wide in a glorious stretch.

Even during bleak times when all seems lost,
nature can come to your rescue to change your mood.
When you are enveloped by nature's blanket,
you realize that you are never truly alone.

Aching for a Date with Nature

I am aching for a date with nature.
We haven't seen each other in some time.
I have been cooped up in my house
and it's time to get out and see the sights.
I am beginning to miss the things
that I haven't seen in a while.

My favorite activities
usually involve water:
sailing along the Caribbean Sea,
cruising through the Panama Canal,
swimming in the ocean,
canoeing on a lake,
and fishing in a river.

I also enjoy the fresh mountain air,
birds chirping in the trees,
and a refreshing mid-summer breeze.

It's a mental thing
to bask in the joy
that nature brings.

I need to add a little zing
to my aching broken heart
by departing from my residence
for a much-needed nature fling.

Humans in the Wild

Humans in the wild were the original crowd.
They roamed the earth, causing nature to wake.
Their naked bodies pranced about without a shroud,
which sometimes caused them to shiver and shake.

They are just part of nature's bounty
like all the other animals and things.
But no other animal on this earth
causes as much chaos as these superior beings.

It's dangerous with this predator
busting loose and coming through.
So, if you are not a comparable competitor,
you should take shelter before they devour you.

Purple Rain

Purple rain falling from the sky
fills the valley below
with rings of fire.

It is the prince of all rain,
bigger than a spring storm
presiding over its grand platform.

Prince appears to be dancing and singing
while playing an electric guitar
and bellowing out flowery chords.

Bigger than life
in all his glory.
It's sad to see
that his life is over…

Reign on forever, my purple Prince.
You will never be forgotten
and your presence will be
forever felt.

IV: PHILOSOPHICAL & SOCIAL

The weight of the world
isn't on your shoulders only.
Learn to share the load.

-Henry Lee Thomas

All Rise

It's been a long, hard road for many
to be recognized as equal by those who rule.
To be trampled upon and abused is not fun
and has become the norm in our inequality cesspool.

There are those who keep you down
and they frown upon your ability to gain ground.
They want to keep the bulk of the pie
and leave you with the crumbs.

It's time for the world to make amends
by promoting a system built on equality,
capturing the down and out before they fall,
and providing a helping hand to those who do.

It's up to us to make it happen.
We need to change the direction of the tide
and strive to make helping each other a passion
to lighten everyone's load so that we all rise.

Stranger Things Have Happened

Imagine people of all races and ethnicities
living together without strife.

Imagine no one starving
or going without basic human needs.

Imagine no war or conflicts
between groups or countries.

Stranger things have happened…

Mary did have a little lamb.
Turkeys were once worshipped like Gods.
Napoleon was once attacked by a horde of bunnies.
The government poisoned alcohol during prohibition.
President Zachary Taylor overdosed on cherries.
Ketchup was sold as medicine in the 1830s.

So maybe there is hope for the world after all
and we can find an agreeable way to live
in peace and harmony.

Let's make it happen!

The Fallacy of the Wise

Smart people sometimes think
they know more than they really do.
Whether due to cockiness or haste,
their minds can often miscue.

The fallacy of the wise is
that they think they are all-knowing
and they make mistakes when they
don't know their own limits.

The wise should continue to question,
look at things in a new light,
and unencumber their brains
to look at new problems
with a novice's eye.

Don't buy into your own hype.
Foster an open mind
to supplement your learned intellect
and you will find that you will be able
to overcome the fallacy of the wise.

I Dream of a World

I dream of a world where everyone is free
to reach for the stars and to be all they can be;
to equally share the resources for success
and not be held back by those who suppress.

You may think this is a pipedream,
since history gives us no role model,
but success starts with a dream.
The rest is perseverance.

We are all more alike than not,
but we use our small differences
as a reason for division instead
of celebrating them for their uniqueness.

I believe the tide is finally turning
as more of us are beginning to see the light.
It's only a matter of time before we hit our stride
and enjoy a world free of injustice, bias, and hate.

Parents, Stop Blaming Yourselves

Parents, stop blaming yourselves
when your children go to hell.
Whether they end up wealthy,
healthy or carted off to jail,
neither outcome means you have failed.

There are many forces at play
that determine your child's fate.
You can only do what you can
and hope that everything else falls into place.

Give yourself a break and know
that trying to predict how a child will turn out
is like foreseeing which way the wind blows
as it streams through its route.

You don't have a crystal-ball
or absolute control.
You can only point them in the right direction
and pray that they take the right road.

Ode to Rebekah Jones

This is an ode to Rebekah Jones
for developing a dashboard that allows
Floridians to track COVID-19.

She had it up in two hours
after it was requested by
the head of Infectious Disease.

The dashboard was an outstanding success,
providing data to see where the cases were
and to make decisions based on it.

But Florida Governor Ron DeSantis
didn't like the dashboard's answers,
so he fired Jones to hide the facts
and to justify his reopening decree.

Floridians paid the price
for DeSantis' villainous act,
as many in the state died.
That should not have been their fate.

But Jones continued to show the truth
out of her allegiance to the people
and not an ambitious leader.

DeSantis put his political aspirations
ahead of public safety,
so it's time
to fire him.

Rebekah Jones: history will be kind to you.
Ron DeSantis: maybe not so much…

To All the Slaves

To all the slaves who died so I could be free:
Your sacrifices were not in vain.
They turned the tide to let freedom ring.

Sometimes it may seem our freedom is fleeting
when there is discontent over our competing
and gaining our share of the pie.

It's a human thing to shun competition;
Survival of the fittest
has been our primary tradition.

But your tenacity has made us strong,
and we will not bow to their game of thrones.
They must understand that equality is the new game.

Some of them have ancestors who were also slaves
and subjected to the same injustices as us.
No one enjoys being in a subjugated role…

The solution is for all of us to have the winning hand
and equally share in all that life has to offer
so that we all can live free.

Real Men Do Cry

It's difficult to define a real man.
There is much debate as to who "he" really is.
One person's definition of a real man
may be another person's worse fear.

In days of old, he was
physically strong, tall, virile,
and he didn't take any crap.

Don't be fooled by these stale rules.
A real man may have those lofty traits,
but more importantly, he is true to himself
and leads life with a moral view.

In case you didn't get the memo:
Real men are sensitive too.
They have real feelings just like everyone else—
and if you were wondering, real men *do* cry.

Stay Woke

Some of us have been
sleeping at the wheel,
thinking that racism had disappeared.
Recent events have shown us
that concept is *not* real.

Wake up, America!
Racism never went away;
It wasn't even hibernating.
The racists have felt more emboldened
to make their case in this time
of divisive rhetoric.

We must stay woke
to combat this disgrace.
If we let our guard down,
we may go up in smoke.

We can't let the racists win.
We need to stay vigilant
and enact counter measures.

When these racists rear their ugly heads,
we must fight back knowing
that truth and justice will prevail.

What If Our Planet Went Extinct?

What if our planet Earth went extinct
and became a dark and empty space—
a black hole in a sky of other stars
where no souls could survive?

Would it matter that we were once great when
there wouldn't be evidence we were in this sphere?
With no way to prove our once diverse empire,
how could one prove that we were ever here?

It wouldn't matter how rich we were.
It wouldn't matter how smart we were.
Our race, color, or ethnicity would not matter.
All our accomplishments would be for naught.
We would all be gone without a trace…

Maybe the possibility of an extinct Earth
will get us to rethink our priorities
and to focus more on elevating our society.
Failing to make this transition,
may make us all null and void.

Honesty

Honesty is not only the name of a flower,
it is also a trait of moral character
with attributes of integrity and trustworthiness.

The flower is called "honesty"
because of its translucent, papery pods.
If we humans would be more translucent,
there would be more honesty and less deceit.

Maybe its human nature to twist the facts
to benefit the self, but no society has survived
for long when everybody fended for themselves.

To benefit the common good and survival of our species,
we need to be more transparent and speak the truth.
If we can achieve this, we will have done a good deed
for our kind and we could be as honest as the flower.

Don’t Forget the Losers

In all races, there are winners and losers.
The winner celebrates and the loser sulks.
The losers leave the scene feeling bruised
when they started the day feeling like the Hulk.

Sometimes, there is very little difference
between the winning score and losing one,
but the impact of the different outcomes
can be as wide as the ocean floor.

In life, we can’t all be winners all the time.
We need to be able to accept losing with grace.
But when there are losers, you can expect discontent.

Don’t forget the losers after celebrating your win.
You need to be sympathetic to their angst and concerns
and incorporate them into your after-win jubilations.
Even though it’s not possible for everybody to win,
you should make it possible that none will suffer.

Love or Hell?

Hell is a four-letter word—
just like love, only hotter.
But when love goes cold,
it can feel like hell.

It can be difficult at times
to determine what state you are in.
Love can be both hot and cold
and hell can feel like a break from the chill
until you begin to feel the heat.

If you are confused about where you are,
it's time to take a step back and observe.
If the heat feels good for your soul, you are in love.
If it feels too hot and suffocating, you are in hell.

Cry Me a Black Man

You were my white girlfriend
and I was your Black man.
I didn't think our difference in race
would cause so much hate.

But you decided to vacate
because you didn't feel safe
with the haters in our wake.

Cry me a Black Man
for believing in fate
and thinking we could mate.

I won't cry over spilled milk
or think about what could have been,
but you are making a big mistake
in not believing in our case.

I don't want to lose you as a friend
and you should find the strength to believe in us.
If we bow down to the haters,
the world can't ascend.

Counterpoint

Should I communicate my thoughts
so others know exactly who I am
or should I sanction them to protect my id?

Should I fall in love
and embrace my passion
or stay aloof and protect my rationality?

Should I dust my brain
with a protective membrane
or should I dust off the rust in my thinking?

Should I enhance my writing
with punctuation to give it a finished look
or trim off the unnecessary words
to make it nice and concise?

Should I clip together
all the things that connect us
or should I clip away all the
things which divide us?

Should I hold up my principle
that all men are created equal
or should I suppress it to maintain the status quo?

Should I screen the examples
of global warming for all to see
or should I screen the devastation from view
and pretend it doesn't exist?

Should I do more
to help eradicate racism
or should I accept that prejudice will endure?

Should I resign my thoughts
that one day we will all be treated equally
or should I sign up to continue to fight the battle?

Should I float the suggestion that we all
should love, respect, and accept each other
or accept that hatred, bias, and disrespect
will always win at the end of each day?

It's a natural fact that there are
multiple ways to deal with an issue.
Which way you choose
makes all the difference.

Philosophical Racism

Many great philosophers held racist beliefs
which were imbedded in their philosophical treatises.
Hume, Hegel, Kant, Locke, and others
all held these racist views on some level.

These flawed views have migrated
into the fabric of our society and has led to:
discrimination of the underrepresented,
unequal treatment by authorities,
and a glass ceiling to higher positions.

Some philosophers believed
that whites operated by reasoning,
while people of color operated by instinct,
posing that non-whites did not have
the mental capacity to project into the future
and could only think about the present.

This racist thought led them to believe that non-whites
are not able to lead complex lives when in fact,
non-whites had their own complex lives and logic,
which were as rich as the European ones.

A philosophy based on systemic racism
leads to a systemic racism of hate.
A philosophy which fails to see
the racism in their speech
is a philosophy of lies.

The fact of the matter is:
We all have the capability for higher thought
and we can all learn from one another.

A diverse group is more likely
to make better choices because
being exposed to more opinions
leads to better decisions.

We need to root out the racism
in our philosophy so we can ascend
to a more accurate philosophical system
because racist philosophy leads to racial injustice.

Being different does not mean being worse;
it just means being different.
Those who do not understand this
are really the ones with limited abilities.

The Soul of Our Country

The soul of our country
lies solely in our hands.
It's up to all of us
to decide where we will land.

We determine the path
by raising our voice
and going to the polls
to register our vote.

We must decide if we
want to treat everyone right
or base our decision on
the color of our skin.

The options are black and white
and there is no in-between.
We can't pretend skin doesn't matter
when the evidence shows otherwise.

At the end of the day,
we all need to realize
that for our nation to survive,
we all must thrive.

Fallen Leaders

Fallen leaders of the past
have created a dictatorial class.
A class of people who seek total control
and are only concerned about their personal goals.

Like Hitler, Mussolini, Noriega, and others,
these dictators ruled by fear and corruption
with desires of being treated like kings.

There appears to be a renaissance of sorts,
where some of the new world leaders
seek to follow in the past dictator's footsteps.

We must be cautious of this new trend;
We know how it worked out before
and shouldn't go down that road again
when we know how it will end…

The world is in a better place
when our leaders follow the Golden Rule
and everyone benefits from their reign.

Unfortunately, some of these leaders
didn't get the memo and are destined
to experience a fall from grace.

Stop the Noise

Noise is what we hear
from all the sounds far and near.
Sometimes, it can be too much for our brain.
Other times, it helps make us sane.

It can be a pathological sound
whose traumatic effects can have no bounds
or it could be a musical tune
that will make us swoon.

But sounds are abounding all over the place,
not allowing us to escape the constant waves.
We are not only experiencing global warming,
global noise is not allowing us
to find a quite space.

It can be hard to live with all this chatter
if it makes it too difficult for us to
focus on things that matter.

Some may feel left out
if there aren't constant sounds around,
but maybe our brains need a break.
It's a noble thing to try to keep abreast
of all that is going on,
but it can get difficult to separate
the information from the noise.

If you give yourself a minute to think,
you will realize:
Sometimes, we just need silence.

Canary in the Coal Mine

Can you hear the canary sing?
There's danger on the horizon,
the world is in disarray,
and there's only so much
we can take.

There is too much conflict to maintain our species.
We are continuing to judge people by their color.
We are not sharing the prosperity of the few.
People are dying and we are acting like
there's nothing we can do.

The canary in the coal mine
is the continued global warming,
the rise in the amount of hate speech,
and the lack of a willingness to compromise.

It is difficult to prognosticate what the future will hold,
but we need to combine our minds to find a solution.
The time to act is now and we have no time to lose.
Let's band together to achieve a common cause,
so we all can survive in harmony and peace.

A Woman in a Man's World

To be a woman in a man's' world
has its ups and downs
when your assets can also be liabilities.

It's a dilemma that men may not grasp
as they are looking up your skirt
while pretending to smell the earth.

How do you balance the pluses and minuses
to ensure you are treated fairly while not
indulging men's primitive urges?

It should not be your problem to fix.
Men need to be held more accountable
and treat women with the respect they deserve.

To Be a Man

To be a man in a "men are dogs" world
can take a terrible toll on your soul.
No matter what move you make,
you are told it's a mistake.

Many accusations are hurled your way
as if you are someone's prey.
No benefit of the doubt,
just a lot of fallout.

It should not be that "Me Too"
implies there is no "He Too".
Equality should go both ways
because that's the American way.

Don't be too quick to pass judgement
when you don't know all the facts.
The "Me Too" movement is long overdue,
but to be a man can be hard too.

If I Were a Woman

If I were a woman,
I would enjoy all the pleasures
that being a woman brings.

I would sit on my throne while being
showered with diamonds and pearls.
I would wear makeup and heels
and be bombarded with free meals.

If I were a woman,
I would probably outlive men.
I'd have more choices in accessories and clothes
and have someone open my door
or give me their seat.

But being a woman
has some liabilities
that many men don't understand,
including sexual assault and backhands.

They are judged more harshly
for their looks.
Looking presentable
takes on a whole new meaning…

Being a woman means
having a glass ceiling, lower wages,
going through painful labor and pregnancy,
and dealing with attitudes from the dark ages.

Who knew that adding “wo” to man
would make such a big difference?
We need to eradicate the unequal treatment
between the sexes and focus on
who the person is.

Deadnaming

It's sad to see
that you won't acknowledge me
by properly addressing me
in the way I want to be seen.

Deadnaming is lame
and it causes me pain.
Why do you insist
on going against my wishes
by using my given name?

Please respect my desire
to be my true self:
the one I identify with,
the one that fits my true spirit.

It's not a complicated thing to have
consideration for my mental health,
so stop impacting my well-being
and call me by my chosen name.

Whose Country Is It Anyway?

There is often talk by an entitled group
in the United States of America
that this is their country
and everybody else
should get out
if they don't
agree with
their *entitled*
views.

If it's anyone's country,
you would have to give it to
all the different Native Americans.
They were here before any others…

This country is founded on the premise
that "All Men Are Created Equal".
So, how do we justify unequal treatment?

The entitled should be united in the cause
to work for the common good of all people.
Instead, they only care about *their* "good"
and they falsely claim that others are "no good".

Though this division exists
in the present place and time,
the truth will eventually lead
us to the correct conclusion:
Regardless of race, sex, ethnicity, or religion,
we all belong in these United States.

The Road to No More

I want to travel along the road to no more.
No more pain, disease, or pandemics.
No more war, fights, or conflicts.
No more famine, thirst, or bad weather.

But if I take the road to no more,
I may miss out on
the road to love, health, and vigor;
to peace and tranquility;
to a world of wealth and prosperity;
and to all that life has to offer.

Sometimes, you must
focus on the good things
to enjoy the whole.
Let's just hope we
can minimize
the sadness…

The Color of History

History has always been painted in the image of the author, and its color is determined by that artist.

Bias present in the artist will be reflected in the history.
When the artist changes, so goes the hue of the history:

- Britain justified taxing the American colonies because they needed money to pay for its war debts.
- The American colonies protested taxation without representation.
- When slavery was in vogue, the historians praised its virtues.
- When slavery was out of vogue, equality and civil rights were the crying call.
- When Whites wrote about the American Indians, the Indians were "savages".
- When the American Indians wrote about their history, they wrote about protecting their land and the Whites' breaking treaties.

History is never just black and white.
There are other colors in the mix.

Write it as it should be written
and don't distort the facts.

If you write it with truth and objectivity,
its true colors will fall in place.

Strange Fruits Dying on the Ground

Strange fruits don't just hang from trees,
they are on the ground begging "please!"
Black bodies soaking up their own blood,
dumped in the dirt to blend in with the mud.

Harvesters firing bullets into Black backs,
telling onlookers they were justifiable acts.
Run down in the street and punched in the teeth,
knees to the neck until they couldn't breathe.

These fruits were not indigenous to this region,
they were forcibly brought here with a large legion.
Once their free labor was no longer an option,
they tried to eradicate them like a dangerous toxin.

Ruling by Fear

Ruling by fear may appear
to be the best way to control.
But the thing about control is
that eventually, all things get out of control.

Many have tried to rule with an iron fist
only to learn that under pressure, it can crack.
At room temperature, everything is fine,
but if the populous gets too hot and bothered,
the temperature slowly rises to a peak
and the ruler begins to feel the heat.

There is a melting point
where the discontent of the population becomes
so high that fear takes a backseat and revolt takes over.
The ruler will then be crushed or ignited by the heat.

Ruling by an iron fist always ends with rebellion.
If you know what the outcome is going to be,
why would you float the iron fist boat?

To enjoy smooth sailing and a happy crew,
try ruling with vision, humility, and integrity.
These are qualities great captains pursue.

The Color Wars

We humans come in many colors.
We also have many traits
and come from many cultures.

From White to Black
along the color track,
our worth is sometimes based
on the lightness of our skin.

Even within the same race,
we tend to judge each other
by our relative hue.

This is a mistake,
which should be relatively clear:
The color of our epidermis
is only a fraction of our makeup.

Our skin color
has no bearing on
our intellect,
our potential,
or our worth.

Maybe we should stop
looking at our skin
and focus on
what's within.

Power

Power in the wrong hands
tends to corrupt the man,
but it depends on who you were
before you got that star.

Some say most men with power
act differently than women with power.
That may be, but the main factor is:
What you were like before you got that gift?

How you act when you have power may be
the same way you would without it.
If you were a jerk beforehand,
maybe you will be a jerk afterwards.
If you were compassionate beforehand,
maybe you will be compassionate afterwards.

Having power reveals your true self:
your values, your vision, your inner self.
Whether you become a dictatorial
or democratic person with power
depends on if you desire to serve or receive.

Be careful who you bestow power to.
If you want to really know who a person is,
give them power and you will find out for sure.

Biased Minds

Biased minds are a sign of the times.
Logic doesn't seem to apply,
and it appears they have
earplugs inside
their ears.

They also have blinders
for glasses so they don't have to see
reality staring at them in the face.

What happened to tolerance, honesty,
open-mindedness, objectivity, compassion,
and the scientific method?

We need to get back to what
really made this nation great:
liberty, equality, and a government for all people
regardless of color or ethnic background.
It's time for those biased minds to lose their power.
It's up to us to make that happen!

Black People without a Cause

Some Black people have achieved the American dream:
money, fame, fancy cars, big house behind a gate,
time to enjoy life and not worry about a thing!

But Black people without a cause
is an accident waiting to happen.
While they are in their false bubble,
they fail to see the outside trouble.

Racism continues to percolate,
waiting for the right time to boil over.
For once those Blacks let their guard down,
their fictitious bubble may begin to burst.

Blacks without a cause
need to support the fight
by advocating for the less fortunate
and helping to push racism back.
If they fail to do their part,
they may find their own fortunes
undergoing an unexpected setback.

Let Pete Rose In

Pete Rose has been denied admittance
to the Baseball Hall of Fame
for betting on a baseball game,
but not on his own team.

There appears to be an inconsistent system of punishment
when some are banished, and others are cherished.
Not that what Rose did was okay,
but he doesn't deserve not to have his "Fame" day.

It is unclear how character and accomplishment
are balanced when determining if someone rates,
but many have made the hall
while exhibiting lower character than Rose.

Does it depend on who you know
or what crowd you run in?
If we are going to have a standard, it should be
equally applied to all without preferential treatment.

Gambling is an illness just like cancer,
drug addiction, mental illness, and other maladies.
Rather than punish, we should treat
and allow people to recover without condemning.

It's time we let Pete Rose in
for all his accomplishments on the ball field—
and if he still suffers from his illness, we should
continue to treat him, but *please let Pete Rose In.*

Vaccinate Me

Many died from COVID-19
after the vaccine hit the streets.
There wasn't enough for everybody,
so who got it first and how were they screened?

People from all over the earth screamed for a vaccine,
especially the ones from the poorest places.
Many died with no one at their side
as they slowly left the scene.

I guess we should be thankful
that the vaccine was developed quickly,
but the distribution of this life-saving elixir
was bungled by the initial man in charge
even after he did a great job getting it ready.

Let's hope that the new man in power is busy as a bee,
getting this medicine out to all to reduce the sobbing.
We are all in need and none of us want to be robbed.
So, let's get it done and somebody, please vaccinate me!

Stupid Lies

Why do intelligent people tell stupid lies,
lies that can clearly be disputed
and ripped to shreds?

How can intelligent people
believe stupid lies when they
have the capacity to know the truth:
The lies calling the Jan 6 Capitol attackers tourists,
Lies about a so called "stolen presidential election",
The lies that the Covid-19 vaccine was ineffective,
Facebook lies.

It shows a lack of critical thinking
to espouse to this nonsense
when your mind should know better.

We need to snap out of it
and let our rational selves take control
before we lose our soul.

Emotional Deficiency

There is a lack of emotional intelligence
in the many peoples of our world.
That is why we are deficient
in our compassion, empathy,
and grace.

Having a high IQ is not enough
to solve the problems
of bigotry, racism
or hate.

It is in our power
to improve the world's fate
by being kind, considerate, thoughtful,
and paying more attention to others' emotions.

If we can achieve this goal,
we will be closer to bringing balance to our
IQ and EQ, ultimately eliminating our emotional deficiency.

We Won't Die

Racism is on its last legs,
and you won't have
a racist leg to stand on
much longer.

The Black equality cause is too strong
to be dethroned by those who are wrong.

We won't die!
No matter how hard you try
to disenfranchise us,
we will still breathe.

You can tear out our guts
into a thousand pieces,
but we will still survive.

You say you are not afraid,
but be afraid,
because it's your days
that are numbered.

Though it is not always the case
that good prevails over evil,
in this instance, it will.
Believe it!

Run while you can.
Time is running out
for false and racist narratives.
You are going down the drain
if you don't get in the right lane.

Life without Purpose

Living the *Life of Riley*
without a care in the world
may seem like the ideal state,
but misery may be in your wake.

While it's important to enjoy the journey
and consume the fruits that life offers,
despair will set in if you don't know
where you are going and your end-goal.

Why you are here is an important question
that you need to answer to have closure.
Going through life aimlessly is no life at all
if you go through it not knowing your cause.

Racism Beans

Racism beans are on the rise.
They are being cultivated by racist lies
by some and planted by many farmers
whose rhetoric cries out “circus performers”.

The beans are being grinded to make a drink,
but once it’s boiled down, it tends to stink.
They mask the taste with powdered sugar,
but it brews hate like a pressure cooker.

It’s time to eradicate these harmful beans
and remove them from our human genes.
If we fail to accomplish this noble cause,
it will violate humanity’s basic laws.

I Thought McCarthyism Was Dead

I thought McCarthyism was dead along with the man himself,
but we are witnessing it again by some in power:
a practice of making accusations of subversion
and false news without proper regard for evidence.

Joseph McCarthy did his best to deceive the public
with his false narratives to attack his enemies.
Margaret Chase Smith was one of the few
senators who tried to beat him back,
but most were afraid of his influence.

Who knew that a contemporary American President
would bring back the McCarthy playbook:
the strategy of labelling one's enemies
with false titles such as communist sympathizer,
socialist, fascist, or unpatriotic.

The troubling thing is that these reckless accusations
are finding more support today than they did before.
There is a surprising number of the political elite
standing on the sidelines or stoking the fires,
intensifying these horrible lies.

This reign of terror must end.
We can't stay silent and let them win.
If we do, it will not be a win
for this country or the world.

Black Lives Do Matter

Thousands of black lives lost,
hanging from a tree.
No crimes committed;
they just wanted to be free.

No gravestone,
no cross,
no obituary
to document the loss…

No regret,
no sorrow,
no justice…

We may never know
who they were.
Their names were lost
when they were taken by force.

They labored for others,
but it was not a labor of love,
because it was done against their will
to enrich their master's purse.

With all the lives lost
and the continuation of this slaughter,
it's time to shout out loud and clear:
Black Lives **Do** Matter!

If You Call Yourself a Christian

If you call yourself a Christian,
you should know what that means.
You should follow the Christian creed
and work on repenting until you succeed.

You should:
show love to all,
not sin if you can help it,
find joy in the little things,
have faith that truth will prevail,
treat your spouse like you care,
have hope when it's not warranted,
show grace to those who need it,
try to take good care of your soul
since that's the only thing
you will have left.

If you can't do these things,
maybe you should
call yourself
something
else?

V: FLASH & SHORT STORIES

Forbidden Fruit

Once upon a time, there were two lonely people named Adam and Eve, whose lives could not have been more different. Everyone knows the story, but most don't know there is another side of it that hasn't been told…

Adam was a handsome man with a strong back and a debonair flair. He would till his garden with vigor, even though the dirt was filled with rocks. He was only able to scratch out a living due to his perseverance and knowledge of the land.

Eve lived in a faraway land with fertile soil and abundant wealth. She had golden brown hair and a goddess stare. She would fill her days with art, music, good food, and beautiful views. But she was bored. She didn't feel like she had a purpose and felt bad that others didn't have it as good as her.

Adam was an educated man, but he worked on the land to help his neighbors and to bring prosperity to the surrounding area. But he soon realized he didn't have the tools to make his goal come true. So, he decided to travel to a faraway place to find the tools he needed to bring wealth to his crew.

Eve decided she needed a break from her unfulfilling life and set out to the east to experience a different view. She and her travel party made their way following the stars at night and enjoying the sites. During a violent storm, she was separated from her mates and aimlessly followed an unknown path, hoping not to end up in an undesirable state.

When the darkness ended and Eve begin to see the light, she noticed a man's figure kneeling over a fire and adding wood to the pile. She slowly approached, hoping for the best. It was Adam and when he looked up, he saw the beautiful stranger looking like an angel. He saw that she was shivering, so he asked if she wanted to come near the fire to warm up. Eve felt the warmth of Adam's smile and settled down next to him, pushing out a nervous grin.

They both noticed they were different races from different lands, but they both felt an attraction and stared at each other for what seemed like days before they began to speak. They quickly realized they had a lot in common and conversed effortlessly about life, the state of the world, and each other.

They spent the next several days getting to know each other and exploring the area. Slowly, they began to fall for each other, sharing their first kiss under a full moon with approving hooting owls and a babbling brook in the background.

As they made their way to Eve's land while holding hands and making plans, they noticed the glances of disapproval surrounding them. The onlookers mumbled, "Who is this outsider with our Eve?"

Eve was pulled aside and told that she was forbidden to consort with Adam because he was not of their kind. But Eve had already tasted the fruit of Adam's love and didn't know if she could give him up after all they had been through and the feelings, she had for him.

Eve knew the decision she made could impact the rest of her life. She asked herself: *Do I give up this great man who has brought me so much happiness, or do I succumb to the pressure and follow the will of my people?*

Eve thought about how unhappy she was before she met Adam and how she was not finding meaning in her life. But she also wondered if she should take a leap of faith that choosing Adam was her destiny.

She looked at Adam and immediately felt his warmth, love, and security. Her decision was made. She handed Adam the lush apple she had hand-picked from the most fertile tree in the Garden of Eden, and he took a bite and handed it back to her. Eve then took a bite and smiled. They held hands and embraced each other, united in their stance of unity, love, and grace.

For their decision, the two lovers were exiled from Eden, but they now had knowledge of good and evil, so they vowed to do their best to promote good and suppress evil.

If you had to make the decision to eat a forbidden fruit, what would you do?

A Race to Remember

Growing up poor in the South means that my social calendar didn't include some of the traditions of the high society. No tea parties, no nights at the opera, no major golf events, and no Kentucky Derby.

I would read about all these functions and the well-heeded people who attended them with their fine clothes and aristocratic flair. They always had a kind of smirk on their face as if to say, "I have it better than you and I am having the time of my life!" I wanted to have *some* of what they had…

I always wanted to attend one of those iconic events of the well-off, such as Wimbledon, the Masters, or the Kentucky Derby, where the air is so rich that you could cut a thin slice of it and payoff your mortgage.

After college, I was able to secure a well-paying position and begin to experience some of the finer things in life. It's interesting to experience two different words: one of modest means and the other of excess. One is not necessarily better than the other if you are able to survive…

I was able to inhale the well-heeded air of the Upper Crust at the International Gold Cup in Great Meadow, The Plains Virginia. It wasn't the Kentucky Derby, but it was close enough.

I had participated in this event twice before, but I had a premonition that the upcoming one would be different.

The International Gold Cup is held every October in the Plains, which is an area in Virginia about an hour west of

Washington, DC. There's also a US Gold Cup in May at the same location.

Besides the horse races, there are also dog races, a best dressed contest, a best hat contest, and other events. These auxiliary events take place in a separate fenced-in area.

The real action, though, is the interactions going on off the field. It's the people-watching, the tailgates, the champagne and caviar, and the ambiance.

During this action-packed circus, I spotted a mare with the most beautiful long brown hair who seemed to gallop in the air and had a smile that momentarily made me stop in my tracks and stare. This was no horse, mind you, but a female human with eyes of blue and freckles too.

She pranced around with delicate care, enjoying the scene with a glass of mint julep in one hand and a flowery hat in the other. I decided to approach her and offer her a refill.

She kindly smiled and said, "Señor, if you can wait until I finish this one, I will have another."

I told her that my name was Enrique, and I would enjoy waiting with her, followed by imploring her to take her time with the one she had because I wasn't in a hurry to depart from her.

I then asked her what her name was.

She replied, "My name is Isabella. Nice to meet you, señor."

I was near my car, so I retrieved a blanket. That way, we could sit on the hill with the good view of the races. Wanting to drink together, I ordered a drink for myself, and we proceeded to descend onto the blanket. I also had one of my poetry books with me, so I asked her if she would like me to read some of my works.

She said, "By all means, señor. Give me your best!"

I said, "Please call me Enrique".

I proceeded to open my book and looked for a piece that fit the moment. But then as our eyes met again, I felt a surge of emotion and out of my mouth came:

Your eyes are daring me to come close.
I open my heart to let you in.
I then close the gate
in case you think
you made a mistake.
But you can see
what's on my mind
and in my heart.

It is you that I desire,
marching next to me
as we hold hands
in our field of dreams.

Let us walk this path
and never look back
as we give into this feeling
of sweet love in the air.

Startled, her eyes opened wide, and her glass was beginning to slip from her hand, so I gently supported her hand to secure the glass in her grip.

She said, "Señor, I mean Enrique, is that one of the poems in your book?"

"No", I replied, "I made it up just for you."

We looked at each other in silence for what seemed like an eternity before I said, "What do you think"?

"I think I am overwhelmed," she confessed.

It was as if the world had stopped and waited for us to make the next move. I knew then that this could not end. I needed to know so much more; I sensed that we had known each other before.

Suddenly, I woke up.

Was it all a dream? What just happened?

I was soaking wet and bewildered as to what the meaning of it all was. She seemed to be so real, this beauty in the field. How tormented I felt that I would never dream of her again…

I looked at my clock and realized that I had to hurry because I needed to shower and get ready to leave for the International Gold Cup. I got ready in a frazzled state and made my way to the race. I was still distraught, but I tried to keep a stiff upper lip.

I meandered around the field aimlessly looking around until I say a lady in the distance sitting on a blanket. As I got closer, I could see her long brown hair flowing in the breeze and her blue eyes with a freckled smile. As I approached with my mouth wide open, she turned to me and looked into my eyes.

“Hello señor Enrique,” she said. “May I have that other drink now please?”

DEFINITIONS

Crime
/krīm/
1. A transgression against harmony that impacts the balance of nature in a negative way.

Emotional Healing
/əˈmōSH(ə)n(ə)l/ /ˈhēliNG/
1. To release the demons in your soul so your spirit can soar.

Family
/ˈfam(ə)lē/
1. A group bound by a gravitational force pulling at their shirttails.

Hate
/hāt/ | [heyt]
1. Irrational brain synapses promulgated by cancerous influences.

Love
/ləv/ | [luhv]
1. Total bliss that at least momentarily filters out all distractions.
2. To be in a suspended animation of orgasmic wonderment.

Orgasm
\ ˈȯr-ˌga-zəm | [awr-gaz-uhm]

1. To be suspended in space and time with sunshine along your back while experiencing a volcanic eruption.

Poetry
po·et·ry | \ ˈpō-ə-trē

1. An expression of feelings in an artistic meter.
2. A grouping of words forming the ingredients of an emotional dish. It can be sweet, bitter, sour, sweet and sour, and many other tastes and aromas.

Pulse
[puhls]

1. The state of the earth, a nation, a relationship, a soul.
2. The thing you check to make sure you are alive.

Relationship
/rəˈlāSH(ə)nˌSHip/

1. The grouping of two or more entities involved in a quid pro quo.

Time
ˈtīm | [tahym]

1. The continuum of our emotional *id* as our life cycles through our psych to satisfy our basic urges, needs, and desires.

ABOUT THE AUTHOR

Henry Lee Thomas is a "*Renaissance man*" whose skills and interests span many areas. He was born in Georgia but has lived in many regions of the United States and traveled throughout the world.

Henry is a poet, engineer, musician, photographer, and observer of life. This diverse background, along with his introspective way of thinking, allows him to see poetry from a unique perspective.

Henry has a B.A. in Mathematics from Oberlin College and an M.S. in Operations Research from the University of Iowa.

Henry Lee's other books include:

The Family Reunion Bible (2021)
978-1-970144-06-2 (P)
978-1-970144-07-9 (H)
978-1-970144-08-6 (E)

Mental Streams (2020)
978-1-970144-03-1 (P)
978-1-970144-04-8 (H)
978-1-970144-05-5 (E)

Poems in the Keys of Life (2019)
978-1-970144-00-0 (P)
978-1-970144-01-7 (H)
978-1-970144-02-4 (E)

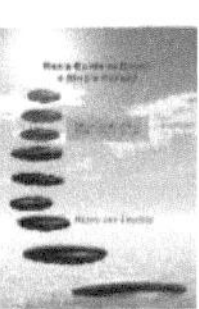

Men's Guide to Being a Single Parent (2014)
978-0615990668 (P)

Photo by Elijah Hiett on Unsplash

Did You Enjoy RISE?

First, thank you for purchasing RISE. I know you could have picked any number of books to read, but you picked this book and for that, I am extremely grateful.
I hope that it added value to your life and was a worthwhile read. If so, it would be really nice if you could share this book with your friends and family by posting to Facebook and/or Twitter.

Also, if you enjoyed this book and found some benefit in reading it, I'd like to hear from you and hope that you could take some time to post a review on Amazon, Barnes & Noble, or any other place of purchase. Your feedback and support will help this author to greatly improve his craft and make his future books even better.

Thank you!

www.ingramcontent.com/pod-product-compliance
Lightning Source LLC
Chambersburg PA
CBHW030610310726
48979CB00003B/647

* 9 7 8 1 9 7 0 1 4 4 1 0 9 *